THE ULTIMATE BALTIMORE ORIOLES TRIVIA BOOK

A Collection of Amazing Trivia Quizzes and Fun Facts for Die-Hard Orioles Fans!

Ray Walker

978-1-953563-54-5

Exclusive Free Book

Crazy Sports Stories

As a thank you for getting a copy of this book I would like to offer you a free copy of my book Crazy Sports Stories which comes packed with interesting stories from your favorite sports such as Football, Hockey, Baseball, Basketball and more.

Grab your free copy over at

RayWalkerMedia.com/Bonus

CONTENTS

INTRODUCTION

The Baltimore Orioles, who were previously known as the St. Louis Browns and Milwaukee Brewers, were established in 1901. No matter their name or where they have been located, they have consistently proven themselves to be a team that fights hard and is a force to be reckoned with in MLB.

The franchise holds three World Series championships, which they won in 1966, 1970, and 1983. They have won seven American League pennants, nine East Division titles, and three wild card berths. They are very often a threat in the American League East Division, having last won it in 2014, with their most recent World Series appearance in 1983.

The Baltimore Orioles have retired Nos. of Cal Ripken Jr., Frank Robinson, Brooks Robinson, Earl Weaver, Jim Palmer, Eddie Murray, and of course, Jackie Robinson, whose number has been retired through MLB.

The Orioles' home is Oriole Park at Camden Yards, which opened in 1992. They play in one of the most difficult divisions in baseball, the American League East, along with the New York Yankees, Boston Red Sox, Toronto Blue Jays, and Tampa Bay Rays.

The thing about baseball is that it's a lot like life. There are good times and bad times, good days and bad days, but you have to do your absolute best to never give up. The Baltimore Orioles have proven that they refuse to give up and that they will do anything they need to do in order to bring a championship to the state of Maryland. Winning is more than possible when you have a storied past like the Baltimore Orioles. They have so much captivating history and so many undeniable player legacies to be profoundly proud of.

With such a storied team past that goes back generations, you're probably already very knowledgeable as the die-hard O's fan that you are. Let's test that knowledge to see if you truly are the World's Biggest Orioles Fan. All facts are up to date as of the end of 2020.

CHAPTER 1:

ORIGINS & HISTORY

QUIZ TIME!

1. Which of the following team names did the Orioles franchise once go by?

    a. Milwaukee Brewers
    b. St. Louis Browns
    c. Baltimore Browns
    d. Both A and B

2. In what year was the franchise established?

    a. 1871
    b. 1881
    c. 1901
    d. 1921

3. The Orioles' current home stadium is Camden Yards.

    a. True
    b. False

4. Which division do the Baltimore Orioles play in?

a. American League East
b. American League Central
c. National League Central
d. National League East

5. The Baltimore Orioles have never won a wild card berth.

a. True
b. False

6. How many American League pennants has the Baltimore Orioles franchise won?

a. 6
b. 7
c. 8
d. 9

7. Who is the current principal owner of the Baltimore Orioles?

a. Larry Dolan
b. Hal Steinbrenner
c. Peter Angelos
d. Arturo Moreno

8. Who is the winningest manager in Baltimore Orioles history?

a. Davey Johnson
b. Paul Richards
c. Buck Showalter
d. Earl Weaver

9. What is the name of the Baltimore Orioles' Triple-A Team and where is it located?
    a. Nashville Sounds
    b. Norfolk Tides
    c. Omaha Storm Chasers
    d. Jacksonville Jumbo Shrimp
10. Who was the first manager of the Orioles' franchise?
    a. Jimmy McAleer
    b. George Sisler
    c. Branch Rickey
    d. Hugh Duffy
11. The Baltimore Orioles were members of the National League East Division from 1969-1993.
    a. True
    b. False
12. What is the name of the Orioles' current spring training home stadium?
    a. CoolToday Park
    b. Spectrum Field
    c. Ed Smith Stadium
    d. Clover Park
13. How many appearances has the Baltimore Orioles franchise made in the MLB playoffs?
    a. 12
    b. 14
    c. 16
    d. 18

14. How many World Series titles have the Baltimore Orioles won?

    a. 1
    b. 2
    c. 3
    d. 5

15. The Baltimore Orioles' current manager is Brandon Hyde.

    a. True
    b. False

16. Which stadium was the first home stadium of the franchise?

    a. Sportsman's Park
    b. Camden Yards
    c. Memorial Stadium
    d. Lloyd Street Grounds

17. Who is the general manager of the Baltimore Orioles?

    a. Mike Rizzo
    b. Mike Elias
    c. David Forst
    d. Nick Krall

18. How many American League East Division titles have the Baltimore Orioles won?

    a. 6
    b. 7
    c. 9
    d. 10

19. The Orioles adopted their team name in honor of the official state bird of Maryland.

    a. True
    b. False

20. John P. Angelos is the CEO and president of the Baltimore Orioles.

    a. True
    b. False

QUIZ ANSWERS

1. D – Both A and B
2. C – 1901
3. A – True
4. A – American League East
5. B – False (They won wild card berths in 1996, 2012, and 2016.)
6. B – 7
7. C – Peter Angelos
8. D – Earl Weaver
9. B – Norfolk Tides
10. D – Hugh Duffy
11. B – False
12. C – Ed Smith Stadium
13. B – 14
14. C – 3
15. A – True
16. D – Lloyd Street Grounds
17. B – Mike Elias
18. C – 9
19. A – True
20. A – True

DID YOU KNOW?

1. The Baltimore Orioles' franchise has had 43 managers: Hugh Duffy, Jimmy McAleer, Jack O'Connor, Bobby Wallace, George Stovall, Jimmy Austin, Branch Rickey, Fielder Jones, Jimmy Burke, Lee Fohl, George Sisler, Dan Howley, Bill Killefer, Allen Sothoron, Rogers Hornsby, Jim Bottomley, Gabby Street, Oscar Melillo, Fred Haney, Luke Sewell, Zack Taylor, Muddy Ruel, Marty Marion, Jimmie Dykes, Paul Richards, Lum Harris, Billy Hitchcock, Hank Bauer, Earl Weaver, Joe Altobelli, Cal Ripken Sr., Frank Robinson, Johnny Oates, Phil Regan, Davey Johnson, Ray Miller, Mike Hargrove, Lee Mazzilli, Sam Perlozzo, Dave Trembley, Juan Samuel, Buck Showalter. and Brandon Hyde.

2. Baltimore's current manager is Brandon Hyde. He played in the Chicago White Sox organization from 1997 to 2000. Hyde previously served as the bench coach, director of player development, and first base coach for the Chicago Cubs, and as a bench coach and interim manager for the Florida Marlins.

3. Earl Weaver is the Baltimore Orioles' all-time winningest manager with a record of 1,480-1,060, for a .582 W-L%. Weaver managed the Baltimore Orioles from 19768 through 1982 and 1985 through 1986.

4. Peter Angelos is the principal owner of the Baltimore Orioles. He is a lawyer as well as a racehorse owner and breeder.
5. The Baltimore Orioles franchise has hosted three MLB All-Star Games so far; in 1948 (Sportsman's Park), 1958 (Memorial Stadium), and 1993 (Camden Yards).
6. Baltimore Orioles pitchers have thrown nine no-hitters. The first occurred in 1912, thrown by Earl Hamilton, and the latest was in 1991, thrown by Bob Milacki, Mike Flanagan, Mark Williamson, and Gregg Olson. As of yet, the Baltimore Orioles have never achieved an elusive no-hitter in their history.
7. The Orioles have an official team hall of fame, located on Eutaw Street at Camden Yards.
8. The Baltimore Orioles' Double-A team is the Bowie Baysox, High Single-A is the Aberdeen IronBirds Low Single-A is the Delmarva Shorebirds.
9. The Baltimore Orioles' mascot is named "The Oriole Bird."
10. The Baltimore Orioles have retired six numbers so far (7 including Jackie Robinson's No. 42, which is retired league-wide). The player who had his number retired most recently was Cal Ripken Jr. in 2001.

CHAPTER 2:
JERSEYS & NUMBERS

QUIZ TIME!

1. The Baltimore Orioles wore alternate sleeveless home uniforms in the 1968 and 1969 seasons.

   a. True
   b. False

2. What are the Baltimore Orioles' official team colors?

   a. Black, orange, and gray
   b. Black, orange, and white
   c. Black, orange, gray, and white
   d. Black, orange, gray, and beige

3. The Baltimore Orioles first wore black uniforms in the 1993 season and have continued to do so ever since.

   a. True
   b. False

4. Which of the following numbers has NOT been retired by the Baltimore Orioles?

a. 1
b. 4
c. 22
d. 33

5. What number does Chris Davis currently wear?

a. 3
b. 9
c. 19
d. 62

6. What number did Jim Palmer wear during his time with the Baltimore Orioles?

a. 11
b. 22
c. 33
d. 44

7. Mike Mussina wore Nos. 35 and 42 during his time with the Baltimore Orioles.

a. True
b. False

8. Rene Gonzales, Paul Carey, and which other player are the only three Baltimore Orioles players have ever worn No. 88?

a. Cesar Valdez
b. Casey Blake
c. T.J. McFarland
d. Albert Belle

9. Who is the only Baltimore Orioles player ever to have worn No. 83?

    a. Robert Machado
    b. Bruce Zimmerman
    c. Justin Turner
    d. Mychal Givens

10. No Baltimore Orioles player has ever won No. 0.

    a. True
    b. False

11. What number did Manny Machado wear as a member of the Baltimore Orioles?

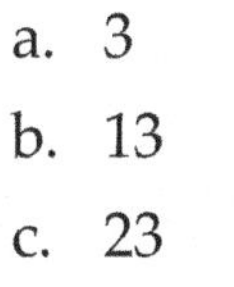

    a. 3
    b. 13
    c. 23
    d. 33

12. What number did Frank Robinson wear as a member of the Baltimore Orioles?

    a. 2
    b. 10
    c. 20
    d. 22

13. Bobby Grich wore Nos. 3 and 16 during his time with the Baltimore Orioles.

    a. True
    b. False

14. What number did Adam Jones wear as a member of the Baltimore Orioles?

    a. 1
    b. 10
    c. 11
    d. 12

15. What number did Mark Belanger wear as a member of the Baltimore Orioles?

    a. 7
    b. 49
    c. 57
    d. Both B and C

16. What number did Brian Roberts wear as a member of the Baltimore Orioles?

    a. 1
    b. 2
    c. 3
    d. 5

17. During his time with the Baltimore Orioles, what number did Eddie Murray wear?

    a. 3
    b. 11
    c. 22
    d. 33

18. What number did Cal Ripken Jr. wear with the Baltimore Orioles?

a. 4
b. 8
c. 18
d. 38

19. What number did Brady Anderson wear as a member of the Baltimore Orioles?

a. 6
b. 9
c. 16
d. Both B and C

20. Paul Blair wore Nos. 6 and 33 during his time with the Baltimore Orioles.

a. True
b. False

QUIZ ANSWERS

1. A – True
2. C – Black, orange, gray, and white
3. A – True
4. A – 1
5. C – 19
6. B – 22
7. A – True
8. D – Albert Belle
9. C – Justin Turner
10. A – True
11. B – 13
12. C – 20
13. A – True
14. B – 10
15. D – Both B and C
16. A – 1
17. D – 33
18. B – 8
19. D – Both B and C
20. A – True

DID YOU KNOW?

1. The Baltimore Orioles have retired seven uniform numbers: Earl Weaver (No. 4), Brooks Robinson (No. 5), Cal Ripken Jr. (No. 8), Frank Robinson (No. 20), Jim Palmer (No. 22), Eddie Murray (No. 33) and Jackie Robinson (No. 42).
2. Eddie Gaedel wore the number 1/8 during his one game with the St. Louis Browns.
3. Boog Powell wore Nos. 8, 16, 26, and 30 during his time with the Baltimore Orioles.
4. During his time with the Baltimore Orioles, Brooks Robinson wore Nos. 5, 6, 34, and 40.
5. During his time with the Baltimore Orioles, Jim Johnson wore Nos. 43, 59, and 64.
6. During his time with the Baltimore Orioles, Miguel Tejada wore Nos. 9 and 10.
7. Jackie Robinson's No. 42 is retired by the Baltimore Orioles as well as the MLB as a whole. No Orioles or MLB player will ever wear No. 42 again. The Yankees' Mariano Rivera was the last player to wear it.
8. During his time with the Baltimore Orioles, Ken Singleton wore No. 29.
9. During his time with the Baltimore Orioles, Don Baylor wore Nos. 23 and 25.

10. During his time with the Baltimore Orioles, Dave McNally wore No. 19.

CHAPTER 3:

AMERICA'S PASTIME

QUIZ TIME!

1. How many total teams play in Major League Baseball?
   a. 15
   b. 20
   c. 30
   d. 33
2. Major League Baseball was founded in 1903.
   a. True
   b. False
3. Who is the current commissioner of Major League Baseball?
   a. Bart Giamatti
   b. Fay Vincent
   c. Bud Selig
   d. Rob Manfred
4. What year was the National League founded?

a. 1870
b. 1876
c. 1903
d. 1911

5. What year was the American League founded?

    a. 1888
    b. 1901
    c. 1903
    d. 1918

6. Major League Baseball is the second wealthiest professional sports league. Which league is the wealthiest?

    a. NBA
    b. NHL
    c. NFL
    d. MLS

7. The Major League Baseball headquarters is located in New York City.

    a. True
    b. False

8. How many games does each Major League Baseball team play per season?

    a. 92
    b. 122
    c. 162
    d. 192

9. In which two U.S. states is Major League Baseball's Spring Training held?

    a. California and Florida
    b. Arizona and Florida
    c. Arizona and California
    d. California and Arizona

10. How many stitches does a Major League Baseball baseball have?

    a. 98
    b. 100
    c. 108
    d. 110

11. Where is the National Baseball Hall of Fame located?

    a. Denver, Colorado
    b. Phoenix, Arizona
    c. Los Angeles, California
    d. Cooperstown, New York

12. All 30 Major League Baseball teams are located in the United States.

    a. True
    b. False

13. Which current Major League Baseball stadium is the oldest baseball stadium still in use?

    a. Angel Stadium
    b. Dodger Stadium

c. Fenway Park
d. Wrigley Field

14. Major League Baseball has the highest attendance of any sports league in the world.

a. True
b. False

15. Fill in the blank: Seventh Inning ______________

a. Jog
b. Song
c. Shake
d. Stretch

16. William Howard Taft was the first United States president to throw out the ceremonial first pitch at a Major League Baseball game.

a. True
b. False

17. It is a Major League Baseball rule that all umpires must wear what color underwear in case they rip their pants?

a. Tan
b. Gray
c. White
d. Black

18. What year did the first Major League Baseball World Series take place?

a. 1903
b. 1905

c. 1915
d. 1920

19. Former Major League Baseball Commissioner, Bart Giamatti is the father of actor, Paul Giamatti.

    a. True
    b. False

20. The song traditionally played in the middle of the 7th inning at Major League Baseball games is called *Take Me Out to the Ballpark.*

    a. True
    b. False

QUIZ ANSWERS

1. C – 30
2. A - True
3. D – Rob Manfred
4. B – 1876
5. B – 1901
6. C – NFL
7. A- True
8. C – 162
9. B – Arizona and Florida
10. C – 108
11. D – Cooperstown, New York
12. B – False, 29 out of 30 (The Toronto Blue Jays are located in Canada)
13. C – Fenway Park
14. A – True
15. D – Stretch
16. A – True
17. D – Black
18. A - 1903
19. A – True
20. B – False, *Take Me Out to the Ballgame*

DID YOU KNOW?

1. The average lifespan of a baseball in a Major League Baseball game is 5-7 pitches. This means approximately 5-6 dozen baseballs are used in every Major League Baseball game.
2. The Boston Americans won the very first Major League Baseball World Series. They defeated the Pittsburgh Pirates in 8 games. Today the most games a World Series can go is 7.
3. The New York Yankees currently hold the most World Series titles in Major League Baseball with 27 total.
4. Hot dogs are the most popular food item sold at Major League Baseball ballparks. Over 21 million hot dogs were sold at MLB stadiums in 2014.
5. The longest Major League Baseball game on record occurred on May 9, 1984 between the Chicago White Sox and Milwaukee Brewers. The game lasted 8 hours, 6 minutes. The most innings played in a Major League Baseball game were 26 innings on May 1, 1920. The game was between the Brooklyn Dodgers and Boston Braves.
6. The mound to home plate distance at Major League Baseball ballparks is 60 feet, 6 inches.
7. Before they can be used in a Major League Baseball game, each MLB baseball is rubbed with a special mud to

improve grip and reduce luster. This special mud comes from a specific, secret location in the state of New Jersey.

8. The fastest Major League Baseball game on record took place on September 28, 1919. The game between the New York Giants and Philadelphia Phillies took 51 minutes. An average MLB game is 3 hours.
9. The American League uses a designated hitter. A DH only hits and does not play in the field. In the National League, the pitcher hits instead of using a designated hitter. If an interleague game is being played, whether a DH is used or not is determined by which team is the home team. If the home team is from the American League, each team will use a DH. If the home team is from the National League, each team's pitcher will hit.
10. The distance between each of the four bases in Major League Baseball is 90 feet.

CHAPTER 4:

CATCHY NICKNAMES

QUIZ TIME!

1. What nickname did Jim Palmer go by?
    a. Pudding
    b. Cakes
    c. Cookies
    d. Muffin
2. Cal Ripken Jr. goes by the nicknames "Iron Man" and "Rip."
    a. True
    b. False
3. Which of the following is NOT a common nickname for the Baltimore Orioles as a team?
    a. The Orange Birds
    b. The O's
    c. The Baltimore Birds
    d. The Birds

4. What nickname does Mike Mussina go by?

   a. Big Mike
   b. Elk
   c. Mussie
   d. Moose

5. "Baby Doll" was a nickname. What was Baby Doll Jacobson's full name?

   a. Charles Joseph Jacobson
   b. Joseph Charles Jacobson
   c. William Chester Jacobson
   d. Chester William Jacobson

6. Which nickname did Mark Belanger go by?

   a. The Hammer
   b. The Slice
   c. The Gun
   d. The Blade

7. Brooks Robinson goes by the nicknames "Human Vacuum Cleaner" and "Mr. Impossible."

   a. True
   b. False

8. "Boog" is a nickname. What is Boog Powell's full name?

   a. Wesley John Powell
   b. John Wesley Powell
   c. Jonathan Wesley Powell
   d. Wesley Jonathan Powell

9. What nickname did Paul Blair go by?

   a. Ballin' Blair
   b. Quick Feet
   c. Motormouth
   d. Baltimore Blair

10. "Buck" is a nickname. What is former Orioles manager Buck Showalter's full name?

   a. Nathaniel William Showalter
   b. William Nathaniel Showalter
   c. Walter Nicholas Showalter
   d. Nicholas Walter Showalter

11. What nickname did Frank Robinson go by?

   a. The Judge
   b. Pencils
   c. The Man
   d. Both A and B

12. Eddie Murray goes by the nickname "Steady Eddie."

   a. True
   b. False

13. Which nickname does Chris Davis go by?

   a. Coca Cola
   b. Crush
   c. Dr. Davis
   d. Seven-Up

14. What nickname did Jim Dwyer go by?

a. Woodstock
b. Snoopy
c. Pig Pen
d. Charlie Brown

15. Don Baylor went by the nicknames "Groove" and "The Sneak Thief."

a. True
b. False

16. What nickname does Jerry Adair go by?

a. Scooby-Doo
b. Yogi Bear
c. Fred Flintstone
d. Casper the Friendly Ghost

17. George Sisler went by the nickname "Gorgeous George."

a. True
b. False

18. What was Jack Powell's nickname?

a. Blue
b. Red
c. Purple
d. Green

19. "J.J." is a nickname. What is J.J. Hardy's full name?

a. Jacob James Hardy
b. Jacob James Hardy
c. James Jerry Hardy
d. Jerry James Hardy

20. Harlond Clift went by the nickname "Darkie."

a. True
b. False

QUIZ ANSWERS

1. B – Cakes
2. A –True
3. C – The Baltimore Birds
4. D – Moose
5. C – William Chester Jacobson
6. D – The Blade
7. A – True
8. B – John Wesley Powell
9. C – Motormouth
10. B – William Nathaniel Showalter
11. D – Both A and B
12. A – True
13. B – Crush
14. C – Pig Pen
15. A – True
16. D – Casper the Friendly Ghost
17. A – True
18. B – Red
19. C – James Jerry Hardy
20. A – True

DID YOU KNOW?

1. Adam Jones has the simple nickname "A.J."
2. Manny Machado has many nicknames. They include Hakuna Machado, Baby Face Assassin, El Ministro de Defensa, and Mr. Miami.
3. Matt Wieters goes by the simple nickname "Wiety."
4. The manager of the Oakland A's, former Oriole Bob Melvin, goes by the nickname "BoMel."
5. Chris Tillman has the nickname "Tilly."
6. Zack Britton's nickname is "Brit."
7. Delino DeShields goes by the nicknames "Bop."
8. Jake Arrieta goes by the nickname "Snake."
9. Ryan Flaherty has the nickname "Flash."
10. Al Bumbry's nickname was "the Bee."

CHAPTER 5:

IRON MAN

QUIZ TIME!

1. What is Cal Ripken Jr.'s full name?
    a. Callum Edwin Ripken Jr.
    b. Calvin Edwin Ripken Jr.
    c. Calvin Edward Ripken Jr.
    d. Callum Edward Ripken Jr.
2. Cal Ripken Jr. played his entire 21-season MLB career with the Baltimore Orioles.
    a. True
    b. False
3. Where was Cal Ripken Jr. born?
    a. Ocean City, Maryland
    b. Baltimore, Maryland
    c. Annapolis, Maryland
    d. Havre de Grace, Maryland
4. When was Cal Ripken Jr. born?

a. April 24, 1960
b. April 24, 1960
c. August 24, 1960
d. August 24, 1970

5. Cal Ripken Jr.'s brother, Billy Ripken, played for the Baltimore Orioles from 1987 to 1992 and in 1996.

    a. True
    b. False

6. How many MLB All-Star Games was Cal Ripken Jr. named to?

    a. 13
    b. 15
    c. 19
    d. 20

7. Cal Ripken Jr. was named the American League Rookie of the Year in what year?

    a. 1980
    b. 1982
    c. 1984
    d. 1986

8. Cal Ripken Jr. did NOT win a World Series championship during his career.

    a. True
    b. False

9. In what year was Cal Ripken Jr. inducted into the National Baseball Hall of Fame with 98.53% of the vote?

a. 2006
b. 2007
c. 2008
d. 2009

10. How many Gold Glove Awards did Cal Ripken Jr. win?

a. 1
b. 2
c. 5
d. 9

11. How many Silver Slugger Awards did Cal Ripken Jr. win?

a. 4
b. 6
c. 8
d. 10

12. Cal Ripken Jr.'s father, Cal Ripken Sr., was manager of the Baltimore Orioles in 1985, 1987, and 1988.

a. True
b. False

13. How many times was Cal Ripken Jr. named the American League MVP?

a. 1
b. 2
c. 3
d. 4

14. Cal Ripken Jr. was inducted into the Baltimore Orioles Hall of Fame in 2003.

a. True
b. False

15. What year did Cal Ripken Jr. win the MLB Home Run Derby?

a. 1990
b. 1991
c. 1993
d. 1995

16. How many home runs did Cal Ripken Jr. hit during his 21-season MLB career?

a. 411
b. 421
c. 431
d. 441

17. Cal Ripken Jr.'s career batting average was .276.

a. True
b. False

18. How many times was Cal Ripken Jr. named the MLB All-Star Game MVP?

a. 0
b. 1
c. 2
d. 3

19. How many times was Cal Ripken Jr. named the MLB Major League Player of the Year?

a. 0
b. 1
c. 2
d. 3

20. Cal Ripken Jr. broke the consecutive games played record on September 6, 1995, in his 2,131st consecutive game.

a. True
b. False

QUIZ ANSWERS

1. B – Calvin Edwin Ripken Jr.
2. A – True
3. D – Havre de Grace, Maryland
4. C – August 24, 1960
5. A – True
6. C – 19
7. B – 1982
8. B – False (He won the World Series championship in 1983.)
9. B – 2007
10. B – 2
11. C – 8
12. A – True
13. B – 2 (He won the award in 1983 and 1991.)
14. A – True
15. B – 1991
16. C – 431
17. A – True
18. C – 2 (He was the All-Star Game MVP in 1991 and 2001.)

19. C – 2 (He won the MLB Player of the Year Award in 1983 and 1991.)
20. A – True

DID YOU KNOW?

1. Cal Ripken Jr.'s wife, Laura is a judge on the Maryland Court of Special Appeals.
2. Cal Ripken Jr. holds the record for most home runs hit as a shortstop (345), breaking the record previously held by Ernie Banks.
3. Since he retired from baseball, Cal Ripken Jr. has purchased three minor league baseball teams.
4. Cal Ripken Jr. holds the MLB record for consecutive games played at 2,632, surpassing Lou Gehrig's streak of 2,130 that stood for 56 years.
5. Cal Ripken Jr. holds 9 MLB records. He also holds 13 Baltimore Orioles records.
6. Cal Ripken Jr. has authored nearly 30 books.
7. On May 31, 2008, Cal Ripken Jr. received an honorary Doctor of Humanities degree from the University of Delaware and served as the university's commencement speaker. On May 19, 2013, he received an honorary Doctor of Public Service degree from the University of Maryland and served as the university's commencement speaker.
8. Cal Ripken Jr. was elected to the National Baseball Hall of Fame in his first year of eligibility with 98.53% of votes.

He was voted in with the sixth-highest election percentage ever.

9. In 2012, Cal Ripken Jr.'s mother, Violet Ripken, was kidnapped at gunpoint and safely returned. In 2013, she was approached by a man with a gun in a parking lot.

10. In 2007, Cal Ripken Jr., along with Andre Agassi, Muhammad Ali, Lance Armstrong, Warrick Dunn, Mia Hamm, Jeff Gordon, Tony Hawk, Andrea Jaeger, Jackie Joyner-Kersee, Mario Lemieux, and Alonzo Mourning founded Athletes for Hope. This charity helps professional athletes get involved with charities and helps inspire people to volunteer and support their communities.

CHAPTER 6:

STATISTICALLY SPEAKING

QUIZ TIME!

1. Cal Ripken Jr. holds the Baltimore Orioles franchise record for the most home runs. How many home runs did he hit?
    a. 411
    b. 421
    c. 431
    d. 441
2. Pitcher Jim Palmer has the most wins in Baltimore Orioles franchise history with 268.
    a. True
    b. False
3. Which pitcher holds the Baltimore Orioles record for most career shutouts thrown with 53?
    a. Mike Cuellar
    b. Jack Powell
    c. Dave McNally
    d. Jim Palmer

4. Which Baltimore Orioles batter holds the single season record for strikeouts with 219?

    a. Mark Reynolds
    b. Chris Davis
    c. Mark Trumbo
    d. Jonathan Villar

5. Jim Palmer has the most strikeouts in Baltimore Orioles franchise history with how many?

    a. 2,112
    b. 2,212
    c. 2,312
    d. 2,412

6. Who has the most stolen bases in Baltimore Orioles franchise history with 351?

    a. Brian Roberts
    b. Brady Anderson
    c. George Sisler
    d. Al Bumbry

7. Gregg Olson holds the record for most saves in Baltimore Orioles history with 160.

    a. True
    b. False

8. Who holds the Baltimore Orioles record for being intentionally walked with 135?

    a. Frank Robinson
    b. Cal Ripken Jr.

c. Eddie Murray
d. Boog Powell

9. Which player holds the Baltimore Orioles franchise record for home runs in a season with 53?

    a. Brady Anderson
    b. Chris Davis
    c. Frank Robinson
    d. Mark Trumbo

10. Which batter holds the single season Baltimore Orioles record for hits with 257?

    a. George Sisler
    b. Heinie Manush
    c. Jack Tobin
    d. Beau Bell

11. Who holds the single season Baltimore Orioles record for double plays grounded into with 32?

    a. Jerry Adair
    b. Miguel Tejada
    c. Cal Ripken Jr.
    d. Brooks Robinson

12. Cal Ripken Jr. holds the franchise record for the most sacrifice flies with 127.

    a. True
    b. False

13. Jim Palmer threw the most wild pitches in Baltimore Orioles franchise history by throwing how many?

a. 65
b. 75
c. 85
d. 95

14. Heinie Manush and George Stone are tied for the Baltimore Orioles single season record for most triples. How many did they each hit?

a. 20
b. 21
c. 22
d. 26

15. Which hitter has the most walks in Baltimore Orioles franchise history with 1,129?

a. Ken Singleton
b. Boog Powell
c. Harlond Clift
d. Cal Ripken Jr.

16. Which hitter holds the franchise record for best overall batting average at .362?

a. George Sisler
b. Heinie Manush
c. Roberto Alomar
d. Ken Williams

17. Cal Ripken Jr. holds the Baltimore Orioles record for most runs scored with 1,647.

a. True
b. False

18. Cal Ripken Jr. has the most plate appearances all time in franchise history with how many?

    a. 9, 883
    b. 10, 883
    c. 11, 883
    d. 12,883

19. Which pitcher holds the Baltimore Orioles franchise record for most saves in a season with 51?

    a. Zack Britton
    b. Jim Johnson
    c. Randy Myers
    d. Gregg Olson

20. Jim Palmer holds the Baltimore Orioles franchise record for most losses with 152.

    a. True
    b. False

QUIZ ANSWERS

1. C – 431
2. A – True
3. D – Jim Palmer
4. B – Chris Davis (2016)
5. B – 2,212
6. C – George Sisler
7. A – True
8. C – Eddie Murray
9. B – Chris Davis (2013)
10. A – George Sisler (1920)
11. C – Cal Ripken Jr. (1985)
12. A – True
13. C – 85
14. A – 20 (Stone in 1906, Manush in 1928)
15. D – Cal Ripken Jr.
16. B – Heinie Manush
17. A – True
18. D – 12,883
19. B – Jim Johnson (2012)
20. A – True

DID YOU KNOW?

1. Jim Palmer threw the most innings in Baltimore Orioles franchise history with 3,948.0. Coming in second is Dave McNally, who threw 2,652.2 innings.

2. George Sisler had the best single season batting average in franchise history at .420 in 1922. Sisler is also second with .407 in 1920.

3. Corey Patterson holds the Baltimore Orioles franchise record for stolen base percentage with 82.40% success. George Sisler holds the Baltimore Orioles franchise record for stolen bases with 351. George Sisler also holds the Baltimore Orioles franchise record for the most times caught stealing at 126 times.

4. Cal Ripken Jr. has the most extra-base hits in Baltimore Orioles franchise history, with 1,078. Second on the list is Brooks Robinson, with 818.

5. Jim Gentile holds the Baltimore Orioles franchise record for at-bats per home run at 15.4. This means that, on average, Gentile hit a home run about every 15-16 at-bats.

6. Dylan Bundy holds the Baltimore Orioles franchise record for strikeouts per 9 innings pitched at 8.819 This means that, during his time with the Orioles, Bundy recorded about 8-9 strikeouts in every 9 innings that he pitched.

7. Brady Anderson holds the single season Baltimore Orioles record for the most hit by pitches with 24 in 1999. Barney Pelty holds the single season Baltimore Orioles record for most batters hit with 20 in 1904.
8. Cal Ripken Jr. holds the Baltimore Orioles franchise record for doubles with 603. Second on the list is Brooks Robinson with 482.
9. Urban Shocker holds the Baltimore Orioles single season record for wins with 27 in 1921. Fred Glade holds the Baltimore Orioles single season record for most losses with 25 in 1905.
10. Gregg Olson holds the Baltimore Orioles franchise record for most saves with 160.

CHAPTER 7:
THE TRADE MARKET

QUIZ TIME!

1. On December 9, 1965, the Baltimore Orioles traded Jack Baldschun, Milt Pappas, and Dick Simpson to which team for Frank Robinson?

   a. Cleveland Indians
   b. California Angels
   c. Los Angeles Dodgers
   d. Cincinnati Reds

2. On June 15, 1976, the Orioles traded Doyle Alexander, Jimmy Freeman, Elrod Hendricks, Ken Holtzman, and Grant Jackson to the which team in exchange for Rick Dempsey, Tippy Martinez, Rudy May, Scott McGregor, and Dave Pagan?

   a. Oakland A's
   b. New York Yankees
   c. Chicago Cubs
   d. Minnesota Twins

3. The Baltimore Orioles have made five trades with the Arizona Diamondbacks as of the end of the 2020 season.

   a. True
   b. False

4. On February 8, 2008, the Baltimore Orioles traded Erik Bedard to which team for Adam Jones, George Sherrill, Chris Tillman, Kam Mickolio, and Tony Butler.

   a. Arizona Diamondbacks
   b. Tampa Bay Rays
   c. Seattle Mariners
   d. Pittsburgh Pirates

5. The Baltimore Orioles have made nine trades with the Colorado Rockies all time (as of the end of 2020).

   a. True
   b. False

6. On December 4, 1968, the Baltimore Orioles traded Curt Blefary and John Mason to which team for Mike Cuellar, Enzo Hernandez, and Tom Johnson?

   a. St. Louis Cardinals
   b. Houston Astros
   c. Oakland A's
   d. New York Yankees

7. On January 10, 1991, the Baltimore Orioles traded Pete Harnisch, Curt Schilling, and Steve Finley to the Houston Astros for which player?

   a. Bob Melvin
   b. Randy Milligan

c. Sam Horn
d. Glenn Davis

8. On December 4, 1974, the Orioles traded Dave McNally, Rich Coggins, and Bill Kirkpatrick to which team for Ken Singleton and Mike Torrez?

   a. Atlanta Braves
   b. Texas Rangers
   c. Montreal Expos
   d. Detroit Tigers

9. On July 18, 2018, the Baltimore Orioles traded which player to the Los Angeles Dodgers in exchange for Yusniel Diaz, Dean Kremer, Zach Pop, Breyvic Valera, and Rylan Bannon?

   a. Adam Jones
   b. Manny Machado
   c. Mark Trumbo
   d. Jonathan Villar

10. The Baltimore Orioles have made only eight trades with the Florida/Miami Marlins all time.

    a. True
    b. False

11. On July 29, 1988, the Baltimore Orioles traded Mike Boddicker to the Boston Red Sox in exchange for Brady Anderson and which player?

    a. Bob Milacki
    b. Don Aase

c. Curt Schilling
d. Gregg Olson

12. The Baltimore Orioles have made only nine trades with the San Diego Padres all time.

a. True
b. False

13. How many trades have the Baltimore Orioles made with the Atlanta Braves all time?

a. 18
b. 20
c. 23
d. 26

14. The Baltimore Orioles have made only eight trades with the Toronto Blue Jays all.

a. True
b. False

15. On July 30, 2011, the Baltimore Orioles traded Koji Uehara to which team in exchange for Chris Davis and Tommy Hunter?

a. Chicago Cubs
b. Boston Red Sox
c. Texas Rangers
d. Tampa Bay Rays

16. On November 17, 1954, the Baltimore Orioles traded Don Larsen, Bob Turley, Billy Hunter, Mike Blyzka, Darrell Johnson, Jim Fridley, and Dick Kryhoski to which team

in exchange for Gus Triandos, Gene Woodling, Willy Miranda, Hal Smith, Jim McDonald, Harry Byrd, Bill Miller, Kal Segrist, Don Leppert, and Theodore Del Guercio.

a. Cleveland Indians
b. New York Yankees
c. Brooklyn Dodgers
d. Chicago White Sox

17. On January 28, 1982. the Orioles traded Doug DeCinces and Jeff Schneider to which team for Dan Ford?

a. Minnesota Twins
b. St. Louis Cardinals
c. California Angels
d. Oakland A's

18. On December 4, 1988, the Orioles traded Eddie Murray to which team for Juan Bell, Brian Holton, and Ken Howell?

a. Cleveland Indians
b. Anaheim Angels
c. New York Mets
d. Los Angeles Dodgers

19. On February 25, 1975, the Baltimore Orioles traded Boog Powell and Don Hood to which team for Alvin McGrew and Dave Duncan?

a. Kansas City Royals
b. Los Angeles Dodgers
c. Cleveland Indians
d. St. Louis Cardinals

20. The Baltimore Orioles have made five trades with the Tampa Bay Rays/Devil Rays all time.

    a. True
    b. False

QUIZ ANSWERS

1. D – Cincinnati Reds
2. B – New York Yankees
3. A – True
4. C – Seattle Mariners
5. A – True
6. B – Houston Astros
7. D – Glenn Davis
8. C – Montreal Expos
9. B – Manny Machado
10. A – True
11. C – Curt Schilling
12. B – False (They have made 19 trades with the Padres.)
13. D – 26
14. A – True
15. C – Texas Rangers
16. B – New York Yankees
17. C – California Angels
18. D – Los Angeles Angels
19. C – Cleveland Indians
20. A – True

DID YOU KNOW?

1. On July 28, 2000, the Baltimore Orioles traded Mike Bordick to the New York Mets in exchange for Melvin Mora, Pat Gorman, Leslie Brea, and Mike Kinkade.
2. On December 2, 2015, the Baltimore Orioles traded Steve Clevenger to the Seattle Mariners in exchange for Mark Trumbo and C.J. Riefenhauser.
3. On July 24, 2018, the Baltimore Orioles traded Zack Britton to the New York Yankees in exchange for Dillon Tate, Josh Rogers, and Cody Carroll.
4. On February 6, 2012, the Baltimore Orioles traded Jeremy Guthrie to the Colorado Rockies in exchange for Jason Hammell, and Matt Lindstrom.
5. On July 31, 2018, the Baltimore Orioles traded Darren O'Day and Kevin Gausman to the Atlanta Braves in exchange for Brett Cumberland, JC Encarnacion, Evan Phillips, Bruce Zimmerman, and international bonus slot money.
6. On December 11, 1991, the Baltimore Orioles traded Bob Melvin to the Kansas City Royals in exchange for Storm Davis.
7. On November 30, 1972, the Baltimore Orioles traded Davey Johnson, Pat Dobson, Johnny Oates, and Roric

Harrison to the Atlanta Braves in exchange for Taylor Duncan and Earl Williams.

8. On January 20, 1977, the Baltimore Orioles traded Paul Blair to the New York Yankees in exchange for Rick Bladt and Elliott Maddox.
9. The Baltimore Orioles have made 20 trades with the Houston Astros as of the end of the 2020 season.
10. The Baltimore Orioles have made 16 trades with the Kansas City Royals as of the end of the 2020 season.

CHAPTER 8:

DRAFT DAY

QUIZ TIME!

1. Cal Ripken Jr. was drafted by the Baltimore Orioles in the 2nd round of which MLB draft?

    a. 1976
    b. 1977
    c. 1978
    d. 1979

2. Eddie Murray was drafted by the Baltimore Orioles in the 3rd round of which MLB draft?

    a. 1972
    b. 1973
    c. 1974
    d. 1975

3. With which pick overall in the 1st round of the 1990 MLB draft, the Baltimore Orioles selected Mike Mussina?

    a. 5th
    b. 10th

c. 15th
d. 20th

4. With which pick overall in the 1st round of the 2007 MLB draft, the Baltimore Orioles selected Bobby Grich?

   a. 1st
   b. 9th
   c. 19th
   d. 29th

5. In the 10th round of the 1985 MLB draft, which team selected Brady Anderson?

   a. Boston Red Sox
   b. Chicago Cubs
   c. Cleveland Indians
   d. Baltimore Orioles

6. Adam Jones was drafted by which team in the 1st round, 37th overall, of the 2003 MLB draft.

   a. Baltimore Orioles
   b. Atlanta Braves
   c. Seattle Mariners
   d. Arizona Diamondbacks

7. Manny Machado was drafted by the Baltimore Orioles in the 1st round, 3rd overall, in the 2010 MLB draft.

   a. True
   b. False

8. With the 3rd overall pick in the 1st round of the 1967 MLB draft, which team selected Ken Singleton?

a. Montreal Expos
b. New York Mets
c. Baltimore Orioles
d. Boston Red Sox

9. With which pick overall in the 1st round of the 1999 MLB draft, the Baltimore Orioles selected Brian Roberts.

a. 10th
b. 20th
c. 30th
d. 50th

10. Mark Trumbo was drafted by the Anaheim Angels in the 18th round of the 2004 MLB draft.

a. True
b. False

11. Zack Britton was drafted by the Baltimore Orioles in which round of the 2006 MLB draft?

a. 2nd
b. 3rd
c. 6th
d. 10th

12. J.J. Hardy was drafted by the Milwaukee Brewers in the 2nd round of the 2001 MLB draft.

a. True
b. False

13. With which pick overall in the 1st round of the 2007 MLB draft, the Baltimore Orioles selected Matt Wieters?

a. 2nd
b. 4th
c. 5th
d. 8th

14. With which pick overall pick in the 1st round of the 2003 MLB draft, the Baltimore Orioles selected Nick Markakis?

a. 4th
b. 5th
c. 7th
d. 10th

15. Chris Davis was drafted by which team in the 5th round of the 2006 MLB draft?

a. Texas Rangers
b. Baltimore Orioles
c. New York Yankees
d. Los Angeles Angels of Anaheim

16. Chris Tillman was drafted by which team in the 2nd round of the 2006 MLB draft?

a. Baltimore Orioles
b. Houston Astros
c. Florida Marlins
d. Seattle Mariners

17. Jim Johnson was drafted in the 5th round of which MLB draft by the Baltimore Orioles?

a. 1999
b. 2001

c. 2003
d. 3005

18. Steve Pearce was drafted in the 8th round of the 2005 MLB draft by which team?

a. Boston Red Sox
b. Toronto Blue Jays
c. Pittsburgh Pirates
d. New York Yankees

19. Jerry Hairston was drafted in which round of the 1997 MLB draft by the Baltimore Orioles?

a. 5th
b. 7th
c. 9th
d. 11th

20. Delino DeShields was drafted by the Baltimore Orioles in the 1st round, 12th overall, of the 1987 MLB draft.

a. True
b. False

QUIZ ANSWERS

1. C – 1978
2. B – 1973
3. D – 20th
4. C – 19th
5. A – Boston Red Sox
6. C – Seattle Mariners
7. A – True
8. B – New York Mets
9. D – 50th
10. A – True
11. B – 3rd
12. A – True
13. C – 5th
14. C – 7th
15. A – Texas Rangers
16. D – Seattle Mariners
17. B – 2001
18. C – Pittsburgh Pirates
19. D – 11th
20. B – False, Montreal Expos

DID YOU KNOW?

1. Harold Baines was drafted in the 1st round (1st overall) of the 1977 MLB draft by the Chicago White Sox.
2. Rafael Palmeiro was drafted in the 1st round (22nd overall) in the 1985 MLB draft by the Chicago Cubs.
3. Jamie Moyer was drafted in the 6th round of the 1984 MLB draft by the Chicago Cubs.
4. Terry Clark was drafted in the 23rd round of the 1979 MLB draft by the St. Louis Cardinals.
5. Will Clark was drafted in the 1st round (2nd overall pick) of the 1985 MLB draft by the San Francisco Giants.
6. Joe Carter was drafted in the 1st round (2nd overall) of the 1981 MLB draft by the Chicago Cubs.
7. Eric Davis was drafted in the 8th round of the 1980 MLB draft by the Cincinnati Reds.
8. B.J. Surhoff was drafted in the 1st round (1st overall) of the 1985 MLB draft by the Milwaukee Brewers.
9. Harold Reynolds was drafted in the 1st round (2nd overall) of the 1980 MLB draft by the Seattle Mariners.
10. Curt Schilling was drafted in the 2nd round of the 1986 MLB draft by the Boston Red Sox.

CHAPTER 9:

ODDS & ENDS

QUIZ TIME!

1. What hobby does Jake Arrieta work on in his free time?

    a. Knitting
    b. Gardening
    c. Woodworking
    d. Building robots

2. Manny Machado is the brother-in-law of fellow MLB player Yonder Alonso.

    a. True
    b. False

3. Jamie Moyer and his ex-wife Karen were introduced by which famous baseball broadcaster?

    a. Vin Scully
    b. Bob Uecker
    c. Harry Caray
    d. Tim McCarver

4. In 2003 Frank Robinson guest-starred in an episode of which show with MLB legends Ernie Banks and Johnny Bench.
    a. *King of Queens*
    b. *Seinfeld*
    c. *Yes, Dear*
    d. *Everybody Loves Raymond*
5. Jake Arrieta was a groomsman in which MLB player's wedding?
    a. Kris Bryant
    b. Matt Carpenter
    c. Anthony Rizzo
    d. Adam Wainwright
6. In 2008, Joe Carter appeared on an episode of which show?
    a. *Trading Spaces*
    b. *Pros vs. Joes*
    c. *The Real Housewives of Orange County*
    d. *Survivor*
7. Curt Schilling is one of only 11 players born in the state of Alaska to play in the MLB.
    a. True
    b. False
8. Which player has played for more MLB teams than any other player in MLB history?
    a. Reggie Jackson
    b. Edwin Jackson

c. Storm Davis
d. Roberto Alomar

9. Lou Piniella made a cameo in which baseball movie?

a. *Moneyball*
b. *Little Big League*
c. *Fever Pitch*
d. *The Rookie*

10. In the 1970s and 1980s, Boog Powell appeared in more than ten different television commercials for which popular product?

a. Hamburger Helper
b. Coca Cola
c. Miller Lite Beer
d. Hubba Bubba Gum

11. In which sitcom did Brady Anderson make an appearance?

a. *Everybody Loves Raymond*
b. *The King of Queens*
c. *Fresh Prince of Bel-Air*
d. *Sabrina the Teenage Witch*

12. Jim Palmer was nicknamed "Cakes" due to his habit of eating pancakes for breakfast on the days he pitched.

a. True
b. False

13. Adam Jones was the best man at which former Orioles teammate's wedding?

a. Chris Davis
b. Quintin Berry
c. Manny Machado
d. Nick Markakis

14. Manny Machado named his dog "Kobe" after basketball legend Kobe Bryant.

a. True
b. False

15. Delino DeShields' daughter Diamond plays in which professional sports league?

a. NWHL
b. LPGA
c. WNBA
d. NWSL

16. Ken Singleton is a cousin of former NBA player and current Philadelphia 76ers head coach Doc Rivers.

a. True
b. False

17. Vladimir Guerrero's son, Vlad Jr., currently plays for which MLB team?

a. Washington Nationals
b. Los Angeles Angels
c. Oakland A's
d. Toronto Blue Jays

18. Frank Robinson was awarded the Presidential Medal of Freedom by which former U.S. President?

a. George H.W. Bush
b. Bill Clinton
c. George W. Bush
d. Barack Obama

19. In 2019, Eric Byrnes set the Guinness world record for which accomplishment?

a. Fastest 100-meter hurdles wearing swim fins
b. Most holes of golf in a single day
c. Most pull-ups in 24 hours
d. Fastest 50 meters walking on hands with a soccer ball between the legs

20. A species of weevil, Sicoderus bautistai, was named after Jose Bautista in 2018.

a. True
b. False

QUIZ ANSWERS

1. C – Woodworking
2. A – True
3. C – Harry Caray
4. C – *Yes, Dear*
5. B – Matt Carpenter
6. B – *Pros vs. Joes*
7. A – True
8. B – Edwin Jackson
9. B – *Little Big League*
10. C – Miller Lite Beer
11. D – *Sabrina the Teenage Witch*
12. A – True
13. B – Quintin Berry
14. A – True
15. C – WNBA (Chicago Sky)
16. A – True
17. D – Toronto Blue Jays
18. C – George W. Bush
19. B – Most holes of golf in a single day (420 holes)
20. A – True

DID YOU KNOW?

1. At one point in his life, Babe Ruth lived on the site that is now Camden Yards, home of the Baltimore Orioles.
2. In 2012, Jake Arrieta appeared on an episode of the HBO show, *Veep*. In 2017, he appeared in an episode of *Chicago Fire* alongside fellow MLB player Kris Bryant.
3. Former Oriole Kevin Millar co-hosts MLB Network's *Intentional Talk with Chris Rose*. The show began back in April of 2011.
4. Former Oriole (and Cal's brother) Billy Ripken is currently an analyst on MLB Network.
5. Mike Mussina is a crossword puzzle enthusiast and was featured in the 2006 documentary film *Wordplay*.
6. In 2019, Chris Davis set the MLB record for the most consecutive at-bats by a position player without a hit, going 0-for-54.
7. Former Oriole Bob Melvin is the current manager of the Oakland A's.
8. Before his MLB career, Al Bumbry served in the U.S. Army during the Vietnam War and was awarded a Bronze Star.
9. After he retired from the MLB, Steve Barber was employed as a bus driver for the Clark County School

District. He provided transportation for children with disabilities from 15 years.

10. Former Orioles Ryan Flaherty and Nick Markakis are brothers-in-law.

CHAPTER 10:

OUTFIELDERS

QUIZ TIME!

1. Over the course of his 15-season MLB career, Nick Markakis has played for the Baltimore Orioles and which other team?

   a. Los Angeles Angels of Anaheim
   b. Atlanta Braves
   c. Seattle Mariners
   d. Pittsburgh Pirates

2. Adam Jones was named to five MLB All-Star Games.

   a. True
   b. False

3. What year was Frank Robinson inducted into the National Baseball Hall of Fame?

   a. 1981
   b. 1982
   c. 1983
   d. 1984

4. Don Baylor won three Silver Slugger Awards.

   a. True
   b. False

5. How many Gold Glove Awards did Paul Blair win?

   a. 2
   b. 4
   c. 6
   d. 8

6. Former Oriole Brady Anderson played 14 seasons with the Baltimore Orioles, 1 season with the Cleveland Indians, and 1 season with which other team?

   a. New York Yankees
   b. San Francisco Giants
   c. Boston Red Sox
   d. St. Louis Cardinals

7. Don Buford played five seasons with the Baltimore Orioles.

   a. True
   b. False

8. How many MLB All-Star Games was Al Bumbry named to?

   a. 0
   b. 1
   c. 2
   d. 3

9. How many seasons did B.J. Surhoff spend with the Baltimore Orioles?

   a. 6
   b. 7
   c. 8
   d. 9

10. How many World Series championships did Ken Singleton win?

    a. 0
    b. 1
    c. 2
    d. 3

11. Curt Blefary was named American League Rookie of the Year in which year?

    a. 1963
    b. 1964
    c. 1965
    d. 1966

12. Fred Lynn was named the 1975 American League Rookie of the Year.

    a. True
    b. False

13. How many MLB All-Star Games was Boog Powell named to?

    a. 2
    b. 3

c. 4
d. 5

14. How many MLB All-Star Games was Jackie Brandt named to?

a. 1
b. 2
c. 3
d. 4

15. Delino DeShields played for the Baltimore Orioles, Los Angeles Dodgers, Chicago Cubs, St. Louis Cardinals, and what other team?

a. Kansas City Royals
b. Toronto Blue Jays
c. Montreal Expos
d. Philadelphia Phillies

16. How many seasons did Jeff Conine spend with the Baltimore Orioles?

a. 3
b. 4
c. 5
d. 6

17. How many Silver Slugger Awards did Melvin Mora win?

a. 0
b. 1
c. 2
d. 3

18. What year was Vladimir Guerrero inducted into the National Baseball Hall of Fame?

    a. 2016
    b. 2017
    c. 2018
    d. 2019

19. How many Silver Slugger Awards did Sammy Sosa win?

    a. 3
    b. 4
    c. 5
    d. 6

20. Reggie Jackson was inducted into the National Baseball Hall of Fame in 1993.

    a. True
    b. False

QUIZ ANSWERS

1. B – Atlanta Braves
2. A – True
3. B – 1982
4. A – True
5. D – 8
6. C – Boston Red Sox
7. A – True
8. B – 1
9. C – 8
10. B – 1
11. C – 1965
12. A – True
13. C – 4
14. B – 2
15. C – Montreal Expos
16. D – 6
17. B – 1
18. C – 2018
19. D – 6
20. A – True

DID YOU KNOW?

1. Adam Jones spent 11 seasons of his 14-season MLB career with the Baltimore Orioles. He also played for the Seattle Mariners and Arizona Diamondbacks. He is a 5x MLB All-Star, 4x Gold Glove Award winner, and Silver Slugger Award winner.
2. Frank Robinson spent 6 seasons of his 22-season MLB career with the Baltimore Orioles. He also played for the Cincinnati Reds, Cleveland Indians, California Angels, and Los Angeles Dodgers. He is a member of the National Baseball Hall of Fame, 2x MVP, NL Rookie of the Year, Triple Crown winner, a 14x MLB All-Star, Gold Glove Award winner, Batting Title champion, All-Star MVP, Major League Player of the Year, AL Manager of the Year, 2x World Series champion, and World Series MVP.
3. Nick Markakis spent 9 seasons of his MLB career with the Baltimore Orioles. He has also played for the Atlanta Braves. He is a 1x MLB All-Star, 3x Gold Glove Award winner, and Silver Slugger Award winner.
4. Paul Blair spent 13 seasons of his 17-season MLB career with the Baltimore Orioles. He also played for the New York Yankees and Cincinnati Reds. He was a 2x MLB All-Star, 4x World Series champion, and 8x Gold Glove Award winner.

5. Brady Anderson spent 14 seasons of his 15-season MLB career with the Baltimore Orioles. He also played for the Boston Red Sox and Cleveland Indians. He is a 3x MLB All-Star.
6. Don Baylor spent 6 seasons of his 19-season MLB career with the Baltimore Orioles. He also played for the California Angels, New York Yankees, Boston Red Sox, Oakland A's, and Minnesota Twins. He is an MVP, 1x MLB All-Star, World Series champion, 3x Silver Slugger Award winner, and Manager of the Year.
7. Boog Powell spent 14 seasons of his 17-season MLB career with the Baltimore Orioles. He also played for the Cleveland Indians and Los Angeles Dodgers. He is an MVP, 4x MLB All-Star, and 2x World Series champion.
8. Melvin Mora spent 10 seasons of his 13-season MLB career with the Baltimore Orioles. He also played for the New York Mets, Arizona Diamondbacks, and Colorado Rockies. He is a 2x MLB All-Star and Silver Slugger Award winner.
9. Vladimir Guerrero spent 1 season of his 16-season MLB career with the Baltimore Orioles. He also played for the Montreal Expos, Los Angeles Angels, and Texas Rangers. He is a member of the National Baseball Hall of Fame, MVP, 9x MLB All-Star, and 8x Silver Slugger Award winner.
10. Reggie Jackson spent 1 season of his 21-season career with the Baltimore Orioles. He also played for the Oakland A's,

New York Yankees, and California Angels. He is a member of the National Baseball Hall of Fame, MVP, 14x MLB All-Star, 5x World Series champion, 2x Silver Slugger Award, 2x World Series MVP, and Major League Player of the Year.

CHAPTER 11:

INFIELDERS

QUIZ TIME!

1. What year was Cal Ripken Jr. inducted into the National Baseball Hall of Fame?
   a. 2005
   b. 2006
   c. 2007
   d. 2008
2. Brooks Robinson was inducted into the National Baseball Hall of Fame in 1983.
   a. True
   b. False
3. What year was Eddie Murray inducted into the National Baseball Hall of Fame?
   a. 2002
   b. 2003
   c. 2004
   d. 2005

4. How many times did George Sisler win the American League batting title?
   a. 1
   b. 2
   c. 3
   d. 4
5. How many seasons did Bobby Wallace spend with the St. Louis Browns?
   a. 4
   b. 5
   c. 10
   d. 15
6. How many Gold Glove Awards did Mark Belanger win during his 18-season MLB career?
   a. 4
   b. 6
   c. 8
   d. 10
7. Harlond Clift spent 10 seasons with the St. Louis Browns.
   a. True
   b. False
8. How many MLB All-Star Games was Bobby Grich named to in his 17-season MLB career?
   a. 2
   b. 3
   c. 6
   d. 8

9. What year did Manny Machado win an American League Platinum Gold Glove Award?

    a. 2012
    b. 2013
    c. 2014
    d. 2015

10. How many MLB All-Star Games was Brian Roberts named to during his 14-season MLB career?

    a. 0
    b. 1
    c. 2
    d. 3

11. How many home runs did Chris Davis hit during the 2013 season?

    a. 40
    b. 43
    c. 50
    d. 53

12. Davey Johnson won three Gold Glove Awards during his 13-season MLB career.

    a. True
    b. False

13. How many MLB All-Star Games was Rafael Palmeiro named to?

    a. 3
    b. 4

c. 6
d. 7

14. What year was Roberto Alomar inducted into the National Baseball Hall of Fame?

    a. 2008
    b. 2010
    c. 2011
    d. 2012

15. What year was Luis Aparicio inducted into the National Baseball Hall of Fame?

    a. 1982
    b. 1983
    c. 1984
    d. 1985

16. J.J. Hardy spent seven seasons with the Baltimore Orioles.

    a. True
    b. False

17. How many MLB All-Star Games was George Kell named to in his 15-season MLB career?

    a. 7
    b. 8
    c. 9
    d. 10

18. Which of the following teams did former Oriole, Kevin Millar NOT play in his 12-season MLB career?

a. Florida Marlins
b. Los Angeles Dodgers
c. Boston Red Sox
d. Toronto Blue Jays

19. How many MLB All-Star Games was Miguel Tejada named to in his 16-season MLB career?

a. 4
b. 5
c. 6
d. 7

20. Harold Reynolds played his entire 12-season MLB career with the Baltimore Orioles.

a. True
b. False

QUIZ ANSWERS

1. C – 2007
2. A – True
3. B – 2003
4. B – 2 (Sisler won batting titles in 1920 and 1922.)
5. D – 15
6. C – 8
7. A – True
8. C – 6
9. B – 2013
10. D – 53
11. C – 2
12. A – True
13. B – 4
14. C – 2011
15. C – 1984
16. A – True
17. D – 10
18. B – Los Angeles Dodgers
19. C – 6
20. B – False (Reynolds played for the Orioles, Seattle Mariners, and California Angels.)

DID YOU KNOW?

1. Cal Ripken Jr. spent his entire 21-season MLB career with the Baltimore Orioles. He is a member of the National Baseball Hall of Fame, 2x MVP, a 19x MLB All-Star, 2x Gold Glove Award winner, 8x Silver Slugger Award winner, 2x All-Star MVP, 2x Major League Player of the Year, Rookie of the Year, and World Series champion.
2. Brooks Robinson spent his entire 23-season MLB career with the Baltimore Orioles. He is a member of the National Baseball Hall of Fame, MVP, an 18x MLB All-Star, 16x Gold Glove Award winner, World Series MVP, All-Star MVP, and 2x World Series champion.
3. Eddie Murray spent 13 seasons of his 21-season MLB career with the Baltimore Orioles. He also played for the Los Angeles Dodgers, Cleveland Indians, New York Mets, and Anaheim Angels. He is a member of the National Baseball Hall of Fame, Rookie of the Year, 8x MLB All-Star, World Series champion, 3x Gold Glove Award winner, and 3x Silver Slugger Award winner.
4. Mark Belanger spent 17 seasons of his 18-season MLB career with the Baltimore Orioles. He also played for the Los Angeles Dodgers. He is a 1x MLB All-Star, 8x Gold Glove Award winner, and World Series champion.
5. Bobby Grich spent 7 seasons of his 17-season MLB career with the Baltimore Orioles. He also played for the

California Angels. He is a 6x MLB All-Star, 4x Gold Glove Award winner, and Silver Slugger Award winner.

6. Manny Machado spent 7 seasons of his MLB career with the Baltimore Orioles. He has also played for the Los Angeles Dodgers. He currently plays for the San Diego Padres. So far in his career, he is a 4x MLB All-Star, 2x Gold Glove Award winner, Silver Slugger Award winner, and Platinum Glove Award winner.

7. Luis Aparicio spent 5 seasons of his 18-season MLB career with the Baltimore Orioles. He also played for the Chicago White Sox and Boston Red Sox. He is a member of the National Baseball Hall of Fame, Rookie of the Year, 13x MLB All-Star, World Series champion, and 9x Gold Glove Award winner.

8. Miguel Tejada spent 5 seasons of his 16-season MLB career with the Baltimore Orioles. He also played for the Oakland A's, Houston Astros, Kansas City Royals, San Diego Padres, and San Francisco Giants. He is an MVP, 6x MLB All-Star, 2x Silver Slugger Award winner, and All-Star MVP.

9. Rafael Palmeiro spent 7 seasons of his 20-season MLB career with the Baltimore Orioles. He also played for the Texas Rangers and Chicago Cubs. He is a 4x MLB All-Star, 3x Gold Glove Award winner, 2x Silver Slugger Award winner, and Major League Player of the Year.

10. Roberto Alomar spent 3 seasons of his 17-season MLB career with Baltimore Orioles. He also played for the

Toronto Blue Jays, San Diego Padres, Cleveland Indians, New York Mets, Chicago White Sox, and Arizona Diamondbacks. He is a 12x MLB All-Star, 2x World Series champion, 10x Gold Glove Award winner, 4x Silver Slugger Award winner, ALCS MVP, and All-Star MVP.

CHAPTER 12:

PITCHERS AND CATCHERS

QUIZ TIME!

1. What year was Mike Mussina inducted into the National Baseball Hall of Fame?

    a. 2016
    b. 2017
    c. 2018
    d. 2019

2. Jim Palmer spent his entire 19-season career with the Baltimore Orioles.

    a. True
    b. False

3. How many MLB All-Star Games was Mike Cuellar named to in his 15-season MLB career?

    a. 2
    b. 3
    c. 4
    d. 5

4. During his 14-season MLB career Dave McNally played 13 seasons with the Baltimore Orioles and 1 season with what other team?
    a. Boston Red Sox
    b. Philadelphia Phillies
    c. Detroit Tigers
    d. Montreal Expos
5. How many seasons did Steve Barber spend with the Baltimore Orioles?
    a. 7
    b. 8
    c. 9
    d. 10
6. Which of the following teams did Milt Pappas NOT play for in his 17-season MLB career?
    a. Chicago Cubs
    b. Pittsburgh Pirates
    c. Cincinnati Reds
    d. Atlanta Braves
7. Zack Britton was named to two MLB All-Star Games during his time with the Baltimore Orioles.
    a. True
    b. False
8. Mike Boddicker won the American League pitching title in what year
    a. 1982
    b. 1983

c. 1984
d. 1985

9. How many seasons did Tippy Martinez spend with the Baltimore Orioles?

a. 9
b. 10
c. 11
d. 12

10. In what year was Hoyt Wilhelm inducted into the National Baseball Hall of Fame?

a. 1982
b. 1983
c. 1984
d. 1985

11. How many MLB All-Star Games was Stu Miller named to in his 16-season MLB career?

a. 1
b. 2
c. 3
d. 4

12. Gregg Olson was named the 1989 American League Rookie of the Year.

a. True
b. False

13. Mike Flanagan won a Cy Young Award in what year?

a. 1977
b. 1978
c. 1979
d. 1980

14. Steve Stone won a Cy Young Award in what year?

a. 1977
b. 1978
c. 1979
d. 1980

15. How many seasons did Darren O'Day spend with the Baltimore Orioles?

a. 6
b. 7
c. 8
d. 9

16. Scott McGregor spent his entire 13-season MLB career with the Baltimore Orioles.

a. True
b. False

17. How many seasons did Jake Arrieta spend with the Baltimore Orioles?

a. 2
b. 4
c. 5
d. 6

18. How many saves did Jim Johnson collect during the 2012 season?

    a. 48
    b. 49
    c. 50
    d. 51

19. How many MLB All-Star Games was B.J. Ryan named to in his 11-season MLB career?

    a. 0
    b. 1
    c. 2
    d. 3

20. Chris Tillman spent his entire 10-season MLB career with the Baltimore Orioles.

    a. True
    b. False

QUIZ ANSWERS

1. D – 2019
2. A – True
3. C – 4
4. D – Montreal Expos
5. B – 8
6. B – Pittsburgh Pirates
7. A – True
8. C – 1984
9. C – 11
10. D – 1985
11. B – 2
12. A – True
13. C – 1979
14. D – 1980
15. B – 7
16. A – True
17. B – 4
18. D – 51
19. C – 2
20. A – True

DID YOU KNOW?

1. Mike Mussina spent 10 seasons of his 18-season MLB career with the Baltimore Orioles. He also played for the New York Yankees. He is a member of the National Baseball Hall of Fame, 5x MLB All-Star, and 7x Gold Glove Award winner.
2. Jim Palmer spent his entire 19-season MLB career with the Baltimore Orioles. He is a member of the National Baseball Hall of Fame, 6x MLB All-Star, 4x Gold Glove Award winner, 2x ERA Title winner, 3x Cy Young Award winner, and 3x World Series champion.
3. Mike Cuellar spent 8 seasons of his 15-season MLB career with the Baltimore Orioles. He also played for the Houston Astros, St. Louis Cardinals, California Angels, and Cincinnati Reds. He was a Cy Young Award winner, 4x MLB All-Star, and World Series champion.
4. Dave McNally spent 13 seasons of his 14-season MLB career with the Baltimore Orioles. He also played for the Montreal Expos. He was a 3x MLB All-Star and 2x World Series champion.
5. Milt Pappas spent 9 seasons of his 17-season MLB career with the Baltimore Orioles He also played for the Chicago Cubs, Cincinnati Reds, and Atlanta Braves. He was a 3x MLB All-Star.

6. Hoyt Wilhelm spent 5 seasons of his 21-season MLB career with the Baltimore Orioles. He also played for the New York Giants, Chicago White Sox, Atlanta Braves, Los Angeles Dodgers, Cleveland Indians, St. Louis Cardinals, California Angels, and Chicago Cubs. He is a member of the National Baseball Hall of Fame, 8x MLB All-Star, 2x ERA title, and World Series champion.
7. Mike Boddicker spent 9 seasons of his 14-season MLB career with the Baltimore Orioles. He also played for the Boston Red Sox, Kansas City Royals, and Milwaukee Brewers. He is a 1x MLB All-Star, World Series champion, Gold Glove Award winner, ERA title winner, and ALCS MVP.
8. Gregg Olson spent 6 seasons of his 14-season MLB career with the Baltimore Orioles. He also played for the Arizona Diamondbacks, Kansas City Royals, Los Angeles Dodgers, Minnesota Twins, Atlanta Braves, Cleveland Indians, Detroit Tigers, and Houston Astros. He is a 1x All-Star and American League Rookie of the Year.
9. Mike Flanagan spent 15 seasons of his 18-season MLB career with the Baltimore Orioles. He also played for the Toronto Blue Jays. He was a 1x MLB All-Star, Cy Young Award winner, and World Series champion.
10. Tippy Martinez spent 11 seasons of his 14-season MLB career with the Baltimore Orioles. He currently plays for the New York Yankees. He also played for the New York Yankees and Minnesota Twins. He is a 1x MLB All-Star and World Series champion.

CHAPTER 13:

WORLD SERIES

QUIZ TIME!

1. How many World Series championships have the Baltimore Orioles won?
    a. 0
    b. 1
    c. 3
    d. 4
2. How many AL pennants has the franchise won?
    a. 5
    b. 7
    c. 8
    d. 9
3. Which team did the St. Louis Browns face in the 1944 World Series?
    a. Chicago Cubs
    b. Cincinnati Reds
    c. Pittsburgh Pirates
    d. St. Louis Cardinals

4. Which team did the Baltimore Orioles face in the 1966 World Series?

   a. San Francisco Giants
   b. Los Angeles Dodgers
   c. Philadelphia Phillies
   d. Pittsburgh Pirates

5. Which team did the Baltimore Orioles face in the 1969 World Series?

   a. New York Mets
   b. Atlanta Braves
   c. Chicago Cubs
   d. San Diego Padres

6. Which team did the Baltimore Orioles face in the 1971 World Series?

   a. Los Angeles Dodgers
   b. Montreal Expos
   c. San Francisco Giants
   d. Pittsburgh Pirates

7. The Baltimore Orioles faced the Cincinnati Reds in the 1970 World Series.

   a. True
   b. False

8. Which team did the Baltimore Orioles face in the 1979 World Series?

   a. Cincinnati Reds
   b. Pittsburgh Pirates

c. Houston Astros
d. Montreal Expos

9. Which team did the Baltimore Orioles face in the 1975 World Series?

a. Atlanta Braves
b. Pittsburgh Pirates
c. Los Angeles Dodgers
d. Philadelphia Phillies

10. How many games did the 1944 World Series go?

a. 4
b. 5
c. 6
d. 7

11. How many games did the 1966 World Series go?

a. 4
b. 5
c. 6
d. 7

12. The 1969 World Series went five games.

a. True
b. False

13. How many games did the 1970 World Series go?

a. 4
b. 5
c. 6
d. 7

14. How many games did the 1971 World Series go?

    a. 4
    b. 5
    c. 6
    d. 7

15. How many games did the 1979 World Series go?

    a. 4
    b. 5
    c. 6
    d. 7

16. The 1983 World Series went five games.

    a. True
    b. False

17. Who was the manager of the St. Louis Browns during the 1944 World Series?

    a. Fred Haney
    b. Rogers Hornsby
    c. Luke Sewell
    d. Paul Richards

18. Who was the manager of the Baltimore Orioles during the 1966 World Series?

    a. Joe Altobelli
    b. Hank Bauer
    c. Earl Weaver
    d. Frank Robinson

19. Who was the manager of the Baltimore Orioles during the 1969, 1970, 1971, and 1979 World Series'?

    a. Billy Hitchcock
    b. Johnny Oates
    c. Frank Robinson
    d. Earl Weaver

20. Joe Altobelli was manager of the Baltimore Orioles during the 1983 World Series.

    a. True
    b. False

QUIZ ANSWERS

1. C – 3 (The Orioles won World Series championships in 1966, 1970, and 1983.)
2. B – 7 (The franchise won pennants in 1944, 1966, 1969, 1970, 1971, 1979, and 1983.)
3. D – St. Louis Cardinals
4. B – Los Angeles Dodgers
5. A – New York Mets
6. D – Pittsburgh Pirates
7. A – True
8. B – Pittsburgh Pirates
9. D – Philadelphia Phillies
10. C – 6
11. A – 4
12. A – True
13. B – 5
14. D – 7
15. D – 7
16. A – True
17. C – Luke Sewell
18. B – Hank Bauer
19. D – Earl Weaver
20. A – True

DID YOU KNOW?

1. Neither team used air travel for the 1983 World Series. Baltimore and Philadelphia are approximately 100 miles apart.
2. Game 4 of the 1971 World Series was the first World Series game played at night.
3. The 1971 World Series was the first of three consecutive World Series where the winning team scored fewer runs overall.
4. The 1969 World Series was the first World Series that took place in the MLB's divisional era.
5. The 1966 World Series was the last one played before the MLB introduced the Commissioner's Trophy that is still awarded to this day.
6. The 1944 World Series marked the third time in World Series history where both teams shared the same home stadium. It is also the only World Series to this day where neither team was credited with a stolen base.
7. The 1944 World Series took place from October 4 through October 9. The 1966 World Series took place from October 5 through October 9. The 1969 World Series took place from October 11 through October 16. The 1970 World Series took place from October 10 through October 15. The 1979 World Series took place from October 10

through October 17. The 1983 World Series took place from October 11 through October 16.

8. The 1966 World Series MVP was Frank Robinson. The 1969 World Series MVP was Donn Clendenon. The 1970 World Series MVP was Brooks Robinson. The 1979 World Series MVP was Willie Stargell. The 1983 World Series MVP was Rick Dempsey.
9. The 1983 World Series was the last World Series with Bowie Kuhn as MLB commissioner.
10. The 1983 World Series is Baltimore's most recent World Series championship, as well as the franchise's most recent appearance in a World Series.

CHAPTER 14:

HEATED RIVALRIES

QUIZ TIME!

1. Which team does NOT play in the American League East with the Baltimore Orioles?
   a. Boston Red Sox
   b. New York Yankees
   c. Tampa Bay Rays
   d. Cleveland Indians
2. The Baltimore Orioles were in the National League East Division from 1969-1993.
   a. True
   b. False
3. Which team below was once a member of the AL East Division?
   a. Cleveland Indians
   b. Milwaukee Brewers
   c. Detroit Tigers
   d. All of the Above

4. What current American League East team has the most AL East championships?

    a. Boston Red Sox
    b. Baltimore Orioles
    c. New York Yankees
    d. Toronto Blue Jays

5. What is a series with the regional rival, the Washington Nationals, called?

    a. Beltway Series
    b. Battle of the Beltways
    c. I-95 Series
    d. Both A and B

6. In what year did the Orioles and Washington Nationals meet for the first time?

    a. 2006
    b. 2007
    c. 2008
    d. 2009

7. The Orioles and Washington Nationals have NOT met in the postseason.

    a. True
    b. False

8. The Orioles have three World Series championships. How many do the Washington Nationals have?

    a. 0
    b. 1

c. 2
d. 3

9. The Orioles have three World Series championships. How many do the New York Yankees have?

    a. 22
    b. 24
    c. 27
    d. 29

10. The Orioles have three World Series championships. How many do the Boston Red Sox have?

    a. 7
    b. 8
    c. 9
    d. 10

11. The Orioles have three World Series championships. How many do the Toronto Blue Jays have?

    a. 0
    b. 2
    c. 4
    d. 5

12. The Tampa Bay Rays have NOT won a World Series championship (as of the end of the 2020 season).

    a. True
    b. False

13. Which player has NOT played for both the Orioles and the Washington Nationals/Montreal Expos?

a. Vladimir Guerrero
b. Jim Dwyer
c. Delino DeShields
d. Mark Belanger

14. Which player has NOT played for both the Orioles and the New York Yankees?

a. Don Baylor
b. Boog Powell
c. Paul Blair
d. Reggie Jackson

15. Which player has NOT played for both the Orioles and the Boston Red Sox?

a. Brady Anderson
b. Kevin Millar
c. Curt Schilling
d. Brian Roberts

16. The American League East is the only division in MLB to contain a non-American team.

a. True
b. False

17. Which player has NOT played for both the Orioles and the Toronto Blue Jays?

a. Roberto Alomar
b. Jonathan Villar
c. Eddie Murray
d. Mike Bordick

18. Which player has NOT played for both the Orioles and the Tampa Bay Rays?

    a. Ken Singleton
    b. Steve Pearce
    c. Gregg Zaun
    d. Erik Bedard

19. How many AL East Division titles did the Detroit Tigers win before they moved to the AL Central?

    a. 0
    b. 1
    c. 3
    d. 4

20. The Milwaukee Brewers won 1 AL East Division championship before they moved to the NL Central.

    a. True
    b. False

QUIZ ANSWERS

1. D – Cleveland Indians
2. B – False (They have always been in the AL East.)
3. D – All of the Above
4. C – New York Yankees (19)
5. D – Both A and B
6. A – 2006
7. A – True
8. B – 1
9. C – 27
10. C – 9
11. B – 2
12. A – True
13. D – Mark Belanger
14. B – Boog Powell
15. D – Brian Roberts
16. A – True
17. C – Eddie Murray
18. A – Ken Singleton
19. C – 3
20. A – True

DID YOU KNOW?

1. The New York Yankees have the most American League East Division championships with 19 (as of the end of the 2020 season). The Boston Red Sox have 10, the Baltimore Orioles have 9, the Toronto Blue Jays have 6, and the Tampa Bay Rays have 3. The Detroit Tigers, formerly of the AL East, won 3 division titles during their time in the AL East. The Milwaukee Brewers won 1 division championship during their time in the AL East, while the Cleveland Indians didn't win any. The most recent AL East Division champions are the Tampa Bay Rays (2020). The Orioles have not won the AL East since 2014 (as of the end of the 2020 season). The Orioles won the AL East in 1969-1971, 1973, 1974, 1979, 1983, 1997, and 2014.

2. Camden Yards and Nationals Park are approximately 40 miles apart. The Orioles are located in Maryland and the Nationals are located in Washington, DC.

3. It has been claimed by sportswriters that the American League East is the toughest division in the MLB. In the 50 years since it was created, an East Division team has played in the World Series 27 times and 16 of those teams have been crowned the World Series champions.

4. Since the 1995 season, when the wild card was introduced, the AL East has produced 20 out of 31 wild card teams for the American League.

5. When the MLB split into two leagues in 1969, the six teams located in the Eastern Time Zone were placed in the East Division, while the other six were placed in the West division.

6. Luis Ayala, Endy Chávez, Bruce Chen, Delino DeShields, Jim Dwyer, Vladimir Guerrero, Jeremy Guthrie, Jerry Hairston, Jeffrey Hammonds, Cesar Izturis, Edwin Jackson, Dave McNally, Mike Morse, Corey Patterson, Mark Reynolds, Gary Roenicke, Pedro Severino, Ken Singleton, Lee Smith, Lenny Webster, and Matt Wieters have all played for both the Baltimore Orioles and the Washington Nationals/Montreal Expos.

7. Luis Ayala, Steve Barber, Don Baylor, Armando Benitez, Wilson Betemit, Paul Blair, Curt Blefary, Richard Bleier, Zack Britton, Clint Courtney, Rick Dempsey, Scott Erickson, Billy Gardner, Jerry Hairston, Elrod Hendricks, Rich Hill, Ken Holtzman, Don Hood, Harry Howell, Grant Jackson, Reggie Jackson, Darrell Johnson, Don Larsen, Tippy Martinez, Mike McCormick, Bob Melvin, Willy Miranda, Bob Muncrief, Mike Mussina, Johnny Oates, Steve Pearce, Lou Pinella, Jack Powell, Tim Raines, Mark Reynolds, Branch Rickey, Brian Roberts, Gary Roenicke, Urban Shocker, Lee Smith, and Gus Triandos have all played for both the Baltimore Orioles and the New York Yankees.

8. Jerry Adair, Manny Alexander, Brady Anderson, Luis Aparicio, Don Baylor, Erik Bedard, Quintin Berry, Mike

Boddicker, Jim Busby, Bruce Chen, Jim Dwyer, Rick Ferrell, Billy Gardner, Wally Gerber, Lenny Green, Grover Hartley, Rich Hill, Baby Doll Jacobson, George Kell, Javy Lopez, Fred Lynn, Jeff Manto, Bob Melvin, Wade Miley, Kevin Millar, Jamie Moyer, Jay Payton, Steve Pearce, Curt Schilling, Al Smith, Lee Smith, Vern Stephens, Sammy Stewart, Koji Uehara, Danny Valencia, Lenny Webster, Dick Williams, and Ken Williams have all played for both the Baltimore Orioles and the Boston Red Sox.

9. Roberto Alomar, Jose Bautista, Armando Benitez, Mike Bordick, Joe Carter, Scott Feldman, Mike Flanagan, Willie Greene, Cesar Izturis, Kevin Millar, Randy Myers, Corey Patterson, Steve Pearce, Nolan Reimold, B.J. Ryan, Travis Snider, Danny Valencia, Jonathan Villar, and Gregg Zaun have all played for both the Baltimore Orioles and the Toronto Blue Jays.

10. Jose Bautista, Erik Bedard, Ozzie Guillen, Jason Hammel, Jeremy Hellickson, Steve Pearce, Alberto Reyes, Ty Wigginton, and Gregg Zaun have all played for both the Baltimore Orioles and the Tampa Bay Rays.

CHAPTER 15:
THE AWARDS SECTION

QUIZ TIME!

1. Which Baltimore player won the American League MVP Award in 1983 and 1991?
   a. Boog Powell
   b. Billy Ripken
   c. Cal Ripken Jr.
   d. Eddie Murray
2. As of the end of the 2020 season, Buck Showalter is the only Baltimore Orioles manager ever to win the Baseball America Manager of the Year Award.
   a. True
   b. False
3. How many Cy Young Awards did Jim Palmer win during his time with the Baltimore Orioles?
   a. 0
   b. 1
   c. 2
   d. 3

4. Which Baltimore Orioles player most recently won the American League Rookie of the Year Award?
   a. Eddie Murray
   b. Cal Ripken Jr.
   c. Gregg Olson
   d. Manny Machado
5. Who is the only pitcher in Baltimore Orioles history to win the Mariano Rivera AL Reliever of the Year Award?
   a. Jim Johnson
   b. Darren O'Day
   c. Zack Britton
   d. Dylan Bundy
6. Which Baltimore Orioles player won a Silver Slugger Award in 1996?
   a. Eddie Murray
   b. Cal Ripken Jr.
   c. Rafael Palmeiro
   d. Roberto Alomar
7. No Baltimore Orioles player has ever won the MLB Home Run Derby.
   a. True
   b. False
8. Which Baltimore Orioles player was named the DHL Hometown Hero (voted by MLB fans as the most outstanding player in franchise history)?
   a. Cal Ripken Jr.
   b. Eddie Murray

c. Mike Mussina
d. Brooks Robinson

9. Who was the first Baltimore Orioles player to win an American League Gold Glove Award?

    a. Luis Aparicio
    b. Brooks Robinson
    c. Paul Blair
    d. Davey Johnson

10. Who was the first Baltimore Orioles player to win a Silver Slugger Award?

    a. Eddie Murray
    b. Cal Ripken Jr.
    c. Mickey Tettleton
    d. Both A and B

11. Which Baltimore Orioles pitcher won the American League Rolaids Relief Man of the Year Award in 1997?

    a. Armando Benitez
    b. Jesse Orosco
    c. Arthur Rhodes
    d. Randy Myers

12. Boog Powell was named the American League MVP in 1970.

    a. True
    b. False

13. Al Bumbry was named the American League Rookie of the Year in what year?

a. 1971
b. 1972
c. 1973
d. 1975

14. Which Oriole was named the MLB All-Star Game MVP in 2005?

    a. Miguel Tejada
    b. Rafael Palmeiro
    c. Sammy Sosa
    d. Eric Byrnes

15. Brooks Robinson won consecutive American League Gold Glove Awards from 1960 through what year?

    a. 1966
    b. 1967
    c. 1970
    d. 1975

16. Ken Singleton won the 1982 Roberto Clemente Award.

    a. True
    b. False

17. Which player is the only Baltimore Orioles player to win a batting Triple Crown?

    a. Cal Ripken Jr.
    b. Brooks Robinson
    c. Frank Robinson
    d. Eddie Murray

18. Which Baltimore Orioles player won a Silver Slugger Award in 2013?

    a. Chris Davis
    b. J.J. Hardy
    c. Adam Jones
    d. All of the Above

19. Which Baltimore Orioles player was named the 1980 American League Cy Young Award?

    a. Jim Palmer
    b. Steve Stone
    c. Mike Flanagan
    d. Scott McGregor

20. The Baltimore Orioles won the 2012 and 2013 Wilson Defensive Team of the Year Award.

    a. True
    b. False

QUIZ ANSWERS

1. C – Cal Ripken Jr.
2. A – True (Showalter won the award in 2012.)
3. D – 3 (Palmer won the AL Cy Young Award in 1973, 1975, and 1976.)
4. C – Gregg Olson (He was named AL Rookie of the Year in 1989.)
5. C – Zack Britton (He won the award in 2016.)
6. D – Roberto Alomar
7. B – False (Cal Ripken Jr. won it in 1991 and Miguel Tejada won it in 2004.)
8. A – Cal Ripken Jr.
9. B – Brooks Robinson (1960)
10. D – Both A and B (1983)
11. D – Randy Myers
12. A – True
13. C – 1973
14. A – Miguel Tejada
15. D – 1975
16. A – True
17. C – Frank Robinson

18. D – All of the Above

19. B – Steve Stone

20. A – True

DID YOU KNOW?

1. The Baltimore Orioles have had four different players win American League Cy Young Awards in franchise history: Mike Cuellar (1969), Jim Palmer (1973, 1975, 1976), Mike Flanagan (1979), and Steve Stone (1980).

2. The Baltimore Orioles have had 10 different players win Silver Slugger Awards: Eddie Murray (1983, 1984), Cal Ripken Jr. (1983, 1984, 1985, 1986, 1989, 1991, 1993, 1994), Mickey Tettleton (1989), Roberto Alomar (1996), Rafael Palmeiro (1998), Miguel Tejada (2004, 2005), Melvin Mora (2004), Aubrey Huff (2008), Chris Davis (2013), J.J. Hardy (2013), and Adam Jones (2013).

3. The Baltimore Orioles have had six different players named American League Rookie of the Year: Ron Hansen (1960), Curt Blefary (1965), Al Bumbry (1973), Eddie Murray (1977), Cal Ripken Jr. (1982), and Gregg Olson (1989).

4. The Baltimore Orioles have had 17 different players win American League Gold Glove Awards: Brooks Robinson, Luis Aparicio, Paul Blair, Davey Johnson, Mark Belanger, Bobby Grich, Jim Palmer, Eddie Murray, Cal Ripken Jr., Mike Mussina, Roberto Alomar, Rafael Palmeiro, Adam Jones, Matt Wieters, Nick Markakis, J.J. Hardy, and Manny Machado.

5. The Baltimore Orioles have had four different players win the American League MVP Award: Brooks Robinson (1964), Frank Robinson (1966), Boog Powell (1970), and Cal Ripken Jr. (1983, 1991).
6. The Baltimore Orioles have had three different players win the American League Rolaids Relief Man of the Year Award: Lee Smith (1994), Randy Myers (1997), and Jim Johnson (2012).
7. The Baltimore Orioles have had two different players win the MLB All-Star Game MVP Award: Cal Ripken Jr. (1991 and 2001) and Miguel Tejada (2005).
8. The Baltimore Orioles have had three different players win the Lou Gehrig Memorial Award: Robin Roberts (1962), Brooks Robinson (1966) and Cal Ripken Jr. (1992).
9. The Baltimore Orioles have had three different managers win the American League Manager of the Year Award: Frank Robinson (1989), Davey Johnson (1997), and Buck Showalter (2014).
10. The Baltimore Orioles have had four different players win the Roberto Clemente Award: Brooks Robinson (1972), Ken Singleton (1982), Cal Ripken Jr. (1992), and Eric Davis (1997).

CHAPTER 16:

MONUMENT CITY

QUIZ TIME!

1. The first factory of which type, in the U.S., was established in Baltimore?.
   a. Shoe
   b. Soda
   c. Umbrella
   d. Soup
2. Babe Ruth was born in Baltimore.
   a. True
   b. False
3. Which tasty treat was invented in Baltimore?
   a. Milkshake
   b. Snow cone
   c. Cheesecake
   d. Pudding
4. Which writer's Baltimore home was designated as a National Historic Landmark in 1972?

a. Ernest Hemingway
b. John Steinbeck
c. Edgar Allen Poe
d. Mark Twain

5. Which famous rapper attended the Baltimore School for the Arts?

    a. Biggie Smalls
    b. Eminem
    c. Drake
    d. Tupac Shakur

6. Which famous swimmer was born in Baltimore?

    a. Kristin Otto
    b. Ian Thorpe
    c. Michael Phelps
    d. Mark Spitz

7. The United States' first Catholic cathedral is located in Baltimore.

    a. True
    b. False

8. What is the name of Baltimore's NFL team?

    a. Baltimore 49ers
    b. Baltimore Bengals
    c. Baltimore Ravens
    d. Baltimore Buccaneers

9. What is the name of Baltimore's aquarium?

a. Aquarium of the Pacific
b. National Aquarium
c. Shedd Aquarium
d. Aquarium of Maryland

10. Which Baltimore team were a professional basketball team in the NBA from 1949 to 1954?

    a. Bulldogs
    b. Bullets
    c. Falcons
    d. Blue Jays

11. What is the name of the Ravens' current stadium?

    a. M&T Bank Stadium
    b. Paul Brown Stadium
    c. Arrowhead Stadium
    d. State Farm Stadium

12. The first American professional sports organization, the Maryland Jockey Club, was formed in Baltimore in 1743.

    a. True
    b. False

13. How many Super Bowl championships have the Baltimore Ravens won?

    a. 0
    b. 1
    c. 2
    d. 3

14. James Brown once owned the number one radio station in Baltimore.

    a. True
    b. False

15. Which actress was NOT born in Baltimore?

    a. Anna Farris
    b. Julie Bowen
    c. Jada Pinkett Smith
    d. Jennifer Aniston

16. The musical *Hairspray* takes place in Baltimore.

    a. True
    b. False

17. Which current NFL team called Baltimore home from 1953 through 1983?

    a. Las Vegas Raiders
    b. San Francisco 49ers
    c. Indianapolis Colts
    d. Atlanta Falcons

18. What is Baltimore/Washington International Thurgood Marshall Airport's code?

    a. BIT
    b. BWA
    c. TMA
    d. BWI

19. How many Super Bowl championships did the Baltimore Colts win?

a. 0
b. 1
c. 2
d. 3

20. Baltimore/Washington International Thurgood Marshall Airport is the first and only airport in America to have a trail for hiking and biking.

a. True
b. False

QUIZ ANSWERS

1. C – Umbrella
2. A – True
3. B – Snow Cones
4. C – Edgar Allen Poe
5. D – Tupac Shakur
6. C – Michael Phelps
7. A – True
8. C – Baltimore Ravens
9. B – National Aquarium
10. B – Bullets
11. A – M&T Bank Stadium
12. A – True
13. C – 2
14. A – True
15. D – Jennifer Aniston
16. A – True
17. C – Indianapolis Colts
18. D – BWI
19. B – 1
20. A – True

DID YOU KNOW?

1. Baltimore was the first United States city to illuminate its streets in 1816. They used hydrogen gas.
2. The Baltimore Museum of Art is home to the Cone Collection, which has the world's largest collection of Henri Matisse's pieces.
3. In Baltimore, it is against the law to sell chicks or ducklings to a minor within one week of Eater.
4. The first dental school in the world was founded in Baltimore in 1840.
5. In 1829, the B&O (Baltimore & Ohio) Railroad was built. It was the United States' first commercial, long distance railroad.
6. In 1774, the first United States post office system was established in Baltimore.
7. The 40-story Legg Mason Building is the tallest building in Baltimore.
8. During the War of 1812, Francis Scott Key wrote the National Anthem in Baltimore while watching the attack on Fort McHenry.
9. Thurgood Marshall, the first African American Supreme Court Justice, was born in Baltimore in 1908.
10. Baltimore has more statues/monuments than any other city in the United States.

CHAPTER 17:

HUMAN VACUUM CLEANER

QUIZ TIME!

1. What is Brooks Robinson's full name?
    a. Calvin Brooks Robinson
    b. Joseph Books Robinson
    c. Brooks Calvin Robinson
    d. Brooks Calbert Robinson
2. Brooks Robinson played his entire 23-season MLB career with the Baltimore Orioles.
    a. True
    b. False
3. Where was Brooks Robinson born?
    a. Hot Springs, Arkansas
    b. Little Rock, Arkansas
    c. Jonesboro, Arkansas
    d. Jacksonville, Arkansas
4. When was Brooks Robinson born?

a. March 18, 1937
b. March 18, 1927
c. May 18, 1937
d. May 18, 1927

5. Brooks Robinson was named the 1966 MLB All-Star Game MVP.

    a. True
    b. False

6. How many Gold Glove Awards did Brooks Robinson win during his 23-season MLB career?

    a. 12
    b. 14
    c. 16
    d. 18

7. What year was Brooks Robinson inducted into the National Baseball Hall of Fame?

    a. 1979
    b. 1980
    c. 1981
    d. 1983

8. Brooks Robinson was named the 1964 American League MVP.

    a. True
    b. False

9. How many World Series championships did Brooks Robinson win in his 23-season MLB career?

a. 0
b. 1
c. 2
d. 3

10. What year did Brooks Robinson make his MLB debut?

a. 1953
b. 1955
c. 1957
d. 1959

11. How many MLB All-Star Games was Brooks Robinson named to?

a. 12
b. 15
c. 16
d. 18

12. The Baltimore Orioles retired Brooks Robinson's No. 5 on April 14, 1978.

a. True
b. False

13. Brooks Robinson was inducted into the Baltimore Orioles Hall of Fame in what year?

a. 1977
b. 1980
c. 1987
d. 1990

14. Brooks Robinson was named the 1970 World Series MVP.

a. True
b. False

15. How many home runs did Brooks Robinson hit?

a. 258
b. 268
c. 278
d. 288

16. What is Brooks Robinson's career batting average?

a. .247
b. .257
c. .267
d. .277

17. Brooks Robinson is tied with Carl Yastrzemski for the record for the longest career spent with a single team in Major League Baseball history.

a. True
b. False

18. How many at-bats did Brooks Robinson have in his 23-season MLB career?

a. 8, 654
b. 9, 654
c. 10, 654
d. 11, 654

19. How many RBIs did Brooks Robinson collect in his MLB career?

a. 1,257
b. 1,357
c. 1,457
d. 1,557

20. Brooks Robinson attended college at the University of Arkansas at Little Rock.

a. True
b. False

QUIZ ANSWERS

1. D – Brooks Calbert Robinson
2. A – True
3. B – Little Rock, Arkansas
4. C – May 18, 1937
5. A – True
6. C – 16
7. D – 1983
8. A – True
9. C – 2 (He won World Series championships in 1966 and 1970)
10. B – 1955
11. D – 18
12. A – True
13. A – 1977
14. A – True
15. B – 268
16. C – .267
17. A – True
18. C – 10, 654
19. B – 1,357
20. A – True

DID YOU KNOW?

1. Brooks Robinson was named to 18 consecutive All-Star Games and won 16 consecutive Gold Glove Awards during his career.
2. Brooks Robinson met his future wife on an Orioles team flight from Kansas City to Boston in 1959. She was working as a flight attendant for United Airlines. He continued ordering iced teas from her so he could keep talking with her.
3. A Brooks Robinson statue was unveiled at Camden Yards on September 29, 2012.
4. Brooks Robinson was given the 2020 National Baseball Hall Bob Feller Act of Valor Award for his service in the Vietnam War.
5. "Never has a player meant more to a franchise and more to a city than Brooks has meant to the Orioles and the city of Baltimore." – Orioles Historian Ted Patterson
6. In 1982, Brooks Robinson helped start the Major League Baseball Players Alumni Association.
7. In 1961, Brooks Robinson opened the *Brooks and Eddie Robinson's Gorsuch House* restaurant, located near Memorial Stadium.
8. Brooks Robinson started Brooks Robinson Sporting Goods in 1963.

9. Brooks Robinson became a spokesman for Crown Central Petroleum in 1968. He spent over 30 years working with them.
10. In 1974, Brooks Robinson wrote an autobiography entitled *Third Base is My Home.*

CHAPTER 18:

STEADY EDDIE

QUIZ TIME!

1. Where was Eddie Murray born?
    a. Oakland, California
    b. San Francisco, California
    c. San Diego, California
    d. Los Angeles, California
2. Eddie Murray's brother Rich played two seasons in the MLB with the San Francisco Giants.
    a. True
    b. False
3. How many Silver Slugger Awards did Eddie Murray win in his 21-season MLB career?
    a. 1
    b. 2
    c. 3
    d. 4

4. How many Gold Glove Awards did Eddie Murray win?

   a. 0
   b. 1
   c. 2
   d. 3

5. How many MLB All-Star Games was Eddie Murray named to?

   a. 3
   b. 4
   c. 8
   d. 10

6. What year was Eddie Murray inducted into the National Baseball Hall of Fame?

   a. 2001
   b. 2003
   c. 2005
   d. 2007

7. Eddie Murray played his entire 21-season MLB career with the Baltimore Orioles.

   a. True
   b. False

8. What year did the Baltimore Orioles retire Eddie Murray's No. 33?

   a. 1998
   b. 1999
   c. 2002
   d. 2003

9. What year was Eddie Murray inducted into the Baltimore Orioles Hall of Fame?

    a. 1998
    b. 1999
    c. 2002
    d. 2003

10. What year was Eddie Murray named the American League Rookie of the Year?

    a. 1975
    b. 1976
    c. 1977
    d. 1978

11. What was Eddie Murray's career batting average?

    a. .257
    b. .267
    c. .277
    d. .287

12. Eddie Murray was a teammate of Ozzie Smith in high school.

    a. True
    b. False

13. How many home runs did Eddie Murray hit?

    a. 204
    b. 304
    c. 404
    d. 504

14. How many RBIs did Eddie Murray collect?

   a. 1,717
   b. 1,817
   c. 1,917
   d. 2,017

15. How many hits did Eddie Murray collect?

   a. 3,155
   b. 3,255
   c. 3,355
   d. 3,455

16. Eddie Murray did NOT win a World Series championship in his MLB career.

   a. True
   b. False

17. Eddie Murray was the American League home run leader and RBI leader in what year?

   a. 1979
   b. 1980
   c. 1981
   d. 1983

18. How many grand slams did Eddie Murray hit?

   a. 15
   b. 17
   c. 19
   d. 21

19. What year did the Orioles unveil a bronze statue of Eddie Murray at Camden Yards?

    a. 2009
    b. 2010
    c. 2011
    d. 2012

20. Eddie Murray has the most RBI among MLB switch hitters all time.

    a. True
    b. False

QUIZ ANSWERS

1. D – Los Angeles, California
2. A – True
3. C – 3
4. D – 3
5. C – 8
6. B – 2003
7. B – False (He also played for the Los Angeles Dodgers, Cleveland Indians, New York Mets, and Anaheim Angels.)
8. A – 1998
9. B – 1999
10. C – 1977
11. D – .287
12. A – True
13. D – 504
14. C – 1,917
15. B – 3,255
16. B – False (He won a World Series championship in 1983.)
17. C – 1981
18. C – 19
19. D – 2012
20. A – True

DID YOU KNOW?

1. Eddie Murray was born the 8th child of 12.
2. After his playing career ended, Eddie Murray coached for the Orioles, Cleveland Indians, and Los Angeles Dodgers.
3. In the *New Bill James Historical Baseball Abstract* book, Eddie Murray is named the fifth-best first baseman in Major League Baseball history.
4. Eddie Murray is one of six players in MLB history to have both 3,000 career hits and 500 home runs. The others are Hank Aaron, Willie Mays, Alex Rodriguez, Albert Pujols, and Rafael Palmeiro.
5. Union Craft Brewery in Baltimore makes "Steady Eddie," a wheat IPA named after Eddie Murray.
6. Eddie Murray stole 110 bases during his 21-season MLB career.
7. Eddie Murray had 11,336 at-bats in his MLB career.
8. Eddie Murray was named the American League Player of the Month four times and he was named the American League Player of the Week nine times.
9. Eddie Murray collected 1,333 walks.
10. In 2008, Eddie Murray released a charity wine called 'Eddie Murray 504 Cabernet' to honor his 504 career home runs. All proceeds were donated to the Baltimore Community Foundation.

CONCLUSION

Learn anything new? Now you truly are the ultimate Orioles fan! Not only did you learn about the O's of the modern era, but you also expanded your knowledge back to the early days of the franchise.

You learned about the Orioles' origins and their history, including where they came from. You learned about the history of their uniforms and jersey numbers, you identified some famous quotes, and read some of the craziest nicknames of all time. You learned more about the legendary Cal Ripken Jr. You also learned about the Hall-of-Famers Brooks Robinson and Steady Eddie Murray.

You were amazed by Orioles' stats and recalled some of the most famous Orioles trades and drafts/draft picks of all time. You broke down your knowledge by outfielders, infielders, pitchers, and catchers. You looked back on the Orioles' championships and playoff feats and the awards that came before, after, and during them. You also learned about the Orioles' fiercest rivalries, within their division and outside it.

Every team in MLB has a storied history, but the Orioles have one of the most memorable of all. They have won three World

Series championships with the backing of their devoted fans. Being the ultimate Orioles fan takes knowledge and a whole lot of patience, which you tested with this book. Whether you knew every answer or were stumped by several questions, you learned some of the most baffling history that the game of baseball has to offer.

The deep history of the Baltimore Orioles franchise represents what we all love about the game of baseball. The heart, the determination, the tough times, and the unexpected moments, plus the players that inspire us and encourage us to do our best because, even if you get knocked down, there is always another game and another day.

With players like Renato Nunez, Pedro Severino, and John Means, the future of the Orioles continues to look bright. They have a lot to prove but there is no doubt that this franchise will continue to be one of the most competitive teams in Major League Baseball year after year.

It's a new decade which means there is a clean slate, ready to continue writing the history of the Baltimore Orioles. The ultimate O's fan cannot wait to see what's to come for their beloved birds.